Flirting with Danger

Pete Guppy

RISING ★ STARS

SURVIVAL

in association with

NASEN House, 4/5 Amber Business Village, Amber Close, Amington,
Tamworth, Staffordshire B77 4RP

Rising Stars UK Ltd.
22 Grafton Street, London W1S 4EX
www.risingstars-uk.com

Text © Rising Stars UK Ltd.

The right of Pete Guppy to be identified as the author of this work has
been asserted by him in accordance with the Copyright, Design and
Patents Act, 1988.

Published 2009

Cover design: Roger Warham
Cover image: Miguel Angel Muñoz Pellicer/Alamy
Text design and typesetting: Roger Warham
Publisher: Gill Budgell
Editorial consultant: Lorraine Petersen

British Library Cataloguing in Publication Data.

A CIP record for this book is available from the British Library.

ISBN: 978-1-84680-601-8

Printed in the UK by CPI Bookmarque, Croydon, CR0 4TD

Mixed Sources
Product group from well-managed
forests and other controlled sources
www.fsc.org Cert no. TT-COC-002227
© 1996 Forest Stewardship Council
FSC

Chapter

1

Jenny tried lifting the rucksack onto her back, but it was too heavy.

"I keep telling you. You've got too much stuff in there," said her dad.

Jenny hated it when her dad was right. "No, I haven't. I can do it," she said. She tried again, but she couldn't lift it.

"Take some of the stuff out," said her dad. Jenny gave him her best 'drop-dead' look.

"I don't need any help, thank you," she said.

Her dad smiled to himself. He knew it was no good arguing with her.

"I'm off to work. I'll see you later," he said.

As soon as he was out of the house, Jenny emptied her rucksack. Out came three big woolly jumpers, three pairs of jeans, three pairs of shorts, six T-shirts, hair gel, a big wash bag, two towels, a big bottle of shampoo, a make-up bag, and four tins of baked beans.

"I'm going to have to cut down," she said to herself.

This time she put in one thin jumper, one pair of jeans, two pairs of shorts, four pairs of pants, three pairs of socks, three T-shirts, a towel, a small wash bag and make-up bag. At the bottom of the rucksack was a sleeping bag and mat.

In the side pockets she put two small tins of beans, a packet of rice, some pasta, a gas burner and a full water bottle.

Jenny lifted the rucksack onto her back. She fastened the clips and pulled the straps tight. Now all she had to do was walk!

It wasn't easy, and her legs felt like jelly as she took her first steps across the room.

"How am I going to walk up and down the cliffs of Cornwall when I can hardly get across this room?" she asked herself.

But she knew she would have to try. She had promised her best friend, Amrit, that she would go on a backpacking trip with her.

Anyway, she didn't want her dad saying, "I told you so. I said you'd never do it."

Jenny was 15 and stubborn. Her mum said she was headstrong. Her dad said she needed her head looking at!

She kept plodding round the room with her pack on. Then she went upstairs. By the time she got down again, her legs were shaking and her knees were hurting like mad.

"This is going to be hard work," she said, as she stood gasping at the bottom of the stairs. The doorbell rang. It was Amrit, with a smile on her face and a rucksack on her back.

She took one look at Jenny's face and said, "Have you been out running with that pack on your back?"

"Very funny," said Jenny. "One more joke like that and you can walk all the way home again."

Amrit took off her rucksack and stepped inside.

"I don't think I can do this walk," Jenny said,

"Yes, you can. Your pack always seems heavy at first. You'll get used to it," said Amrit. She helped Jenny get her pack off her back.

Jenny said, "It's OK, for you. You've done some backpacking with the school."

"Well, you could have had a go at the Duke of Edinburgh Award as well," Amrit said.

"I didn't fancy any of the boys," said Jenny.

Amrit smiled and said, "Let's check the packs and look at the maps. We need to be ready for tomorrow."

This was when their two families would drive down to Cornwall for a two-week camping holiday by the sea.

It was something they did every summer. There would be lots of games on the beach, swimming, rock pools, sand-castles, kite flying and fish and chips.

They were good holidays and the two girls had been enjoying them since they were seven years old.

But for the last two years, Jenny and Amrit had wanted to have a holiday on their own.

"No. Wait a bit longer," said Amrit's parents.

"You're still too young," said Jenny's parents.

But the girls hadn't wanted to wait. Amrit wanted to see new places. Jenny wanted to meet new boys.

So Amrit came up with a plan. They would go on holiday with their parents, but go backpacking for a few days while they were there.

Jenny soon had her dad agreeing to it. But her mum had said, "Maybe."

Amrit had pleaded with her parents, saying, "I'm doing my Duke of Edinburgh Award. I've got my silver. I've done an overnight camp and I can read a map. I know what I'm doing."

Her mum had said, "Maybe."

But her dad said, "No." After more pleading he'd said, "I'll talk it over with Jenny's dad."

At last, the girls were told they could do it as long as it was well planned. Amrit had done the planning and now they couldn't wait to get down to Cornwall.

Chapter 2

The drive down to Cornwall was long, hot and boring. In Jenny's car, fighting soon broke out between her six-year-old brother and her eight-year-old sister. James dug Vicky in the ribs, so Vicky kicked his shins. James hit her, so Vicky bit him. Three times their dad shouted, "I'll turn this car round if you two don't stop fighting."

The fighting didn't stop, it just went underground for a time.

Mum started counting the number of times James asked, "Are we there yet?" She got to ten and gave up.

Jenny sat listening to her iPod. She sometimes sang loudly, and out of tune, until everyone shouted, "Shut up!"

In Amrit's car, putting newspaper on the seats didn't stop six-year-old Krishan from being sick three times. His five-year-old sister Seema, always wanted to do what he did. So she joined in and was sick twice.

Amrit's dad swore at another car driver, and her mum said, "Shh, not in front of the children."

Krishan knew how he could use this to get his dad into trouble when they got home. He'd say to his grandma, "Gran, Dad told us a new word on the way down to Cornwall."

It would be fun watching his dad panic.

Amrit looked at maps and played games on her Nintendo. Then Krishan and Seema were sick again. After five long hours the sea came into sight. Everyone cheered and the sickness and fighting stopped.

As soon as they got to the campsite, the work began. The children helped by rushing off to the beach with Jenny and Amrit. By the time they came back, the big tents were up and their parents were sitting round a table having a drink.

The holiday had begun. The next few days were spent doing what they always did on these holidays.

Then came the morning Amrit and Jenny had been waiting for. They put on their rucksacks to begin their four-day backpacking trip. Their mums fussed around them and took photographs.

Their dads gave them yet another talk on being careful about cliffs, tides and boys.

Little Vicky said to Jenny, "Be careful you don't walk over any cliffs."

Little Krishan said, "Can I have your iPod if you do?"

They checked their mobiles and were told to ring every morning and evening.

It was time to go. There were hugs and kisses all round, and a small crowd of campers clapped as they set off.

"They will be all right, won't they?" asked Amrit's mum.

"They'll be fine," said Jenny's dad. But they all knew they would feel much happier when they got a call from the girls that evening.

Chapter 3

They were on their own at last, heading for freedom. It was a big step for both of them. But right now, Jenny was only taking small steps and trying not to fall flat on her face.

The two girls stopped at the end of the campsite and turned to wave one last time.

Then they stepped onto the coast path and were soon out of sight.

Amrit walked quickly along the path and Jenny plodded behind her. They were soon too far apart to talk. But talking wasn't what they wanted to do.

Amrit was thinking about how upset her mum had been when they left. She didn't like to see her like that, but there was no turning back. This was the first part of her plan to live her life as she wanted to live it. She wanted to pass her exams, get a job and get a flat of her own. These were all big steps for Amrit and this walk was one of them. She had to finish it.

Jenny was thinking about two things. One, how had she let herself be talked into doing this walk? And two, how could she get out of it? Amrit waited for her at the next bend.

Jenny asked, "Can't we just do a one-day trip? Then we could go back to the campsite for a nice meal tonight."

"We've only been going 20 minutes. You'll soon get used to your pack," said Amrit.

"I'll never get used to this pack. I thought you said backpacking was fun," said Jenny.

Amrit said, "We'll walk for 30 minutes and then have a 5-minute rest. We'll do that until we get to Zennor."

"Where's that?" asked Jenny.

"It's where we're camping tonight," said Amrit.

"How far is it?" asked Jenny.

"Just over 5 miles," said Amrit.

"_____," said Jenny.

Amrit said, "Just look around you as you walk. It'll stop you thinking about your pack."

16

The sea was sparkling in the sunlight.
Waves were crashing onto the rocks.
Sea birds were diving for fish. Kestrels were
hovering in the air and looking for food.

But Jenny didn't see any of that. She just
plodded on, saying in a loud voice,
"If God had wanted me to carry heavy loads,
he'd have given me four legs, not two."

"Stop moaning," said Amrit.

"I'm not moaning. I'm just saying,"
said Jenny.

An hour later, Jenny was too tired to
moan. The coast path kept dipping down to
the sea and climbing up again. It was like
doing 50 P.E. lessons all in one go. Her
lungs felt as if they were bursting, and even
Amrit was gasping for air as they struggled
up the next bit of the path.

"Time for another rest," said Amrit. The
girls dropped their packs on the ground and
flopped down beside them.

Jenny lay flat on her back, gazing up at the clouds drifting by.

"I can't walk another step. My legs have gone on strike. Can't we get a taxi?" she said. Amrit wasn't listening to her. She was looking at something down in the water.

"Come over here, Jenny. Come and look at this," she said.

"I can't. I'm never moving again," said Jenny.

"It's a baby seal with its mum," said Amrit.

Jenny was by her side in a flash.

"Where, where?" she asked, as she hung over the edge of the cliff.

"Down there on that little bit of sand. I'll get my binoculars so we can see better," said Amrit.

The two girls spent 20 minutes watching the seal pup nuzzle up to its mum for milk. It was a great sight.

Then they put on their packs and set off again. Seeing the seals had put a smile on their faces and made them forget how tired they were.

An hour later they stopped to eat their lunch. Jenny took out her mobile.

"I'll give them a call to let them know how we're getting on," she said.

"No," said Amrit, sharply.

Jenny looked puzzled. "Why not? Don't you want to talk to your mum and dad?" she asked.

Amrit said, "I love my mum and dad to bits. But I've got to show them I'm growing up and don't need to talk to them every five minutes. Let's just ring them tonight."

Jenny could see it was important to her, so she put her mobile back in her pack. Then they both stretched out in the hot sun.

"We need to get going soon," said Amrit.

"Yes, soon," said Jenny.

An hour later, Amrit said, "We should be moving on."

"I agree," said Jenny as she rolled over to let the sun get on her back.

Two men with heavy-looking packs came walking past. After they had gone, Jenny said, "Look at those sad old gits. Fancy still going backpacking at their age!"

"They must be as old as our dads," said Amrit.

"That's what I said, sad old gits," said Jenny. They both fell around laughing.

At last, Jenny said, "Come on. Let's get going." There were moans and groans as they started to move their stiff legs again. After two more stops for water, they were heading inland on the path to Zennor.

Chapter 4

As Amrit and Jenny walked into the village, they saw two lads talking to each other. The one sitting on a motorbike had short blond hair and looked about 18.

He took off his sunglasses as they walked by and said, "Hi girls. You two look fit. Fancy a drink later on?"

Amrit didn't say anything.

Jenny looked round and said, "Maybe."

"Result. I've got a date!" he shouted.

He kick-started his bike and roared off up the road in a cloud of smoke and dust.

"Show off," said Amrit.

"Yes, but he's cute," giggled Jenny.

The girls walked on and found a small campsite. It wasn't long before the tent was put up, and they were drinking a cup of tea.

"This is the best cup of tea I've ever had," said Jenny.

Amrit said, "We've got to be careful. We got to a tap just in time. We only had a drop left in our water bottles. We need to take plenty with us every day. You can go miles and not see a tap."

"How do you know that?" asked Jenny.

"It's in the book I've got about this coast path. You've seen it, it's in my pack," said Amrit.

"Talking of drinking, do you fancy seeing those two lads at the pub tonight?" asked Jenny.

"We're too young to drink," said Amrit.

Jenny said, "Yes, I know. But you don't look too young when you've got a bit of make-up on. I do, but you don't. So you could get the drinks and we could sit outside."

"But we don't know them, and I don't trust the one with the motorbike," said Amrit.

"Come on. It could be fun," said Jenny.

"My mum and dad don't agree with under-age drinking," said Amrit.

But Jenny wasn't giving up.

"We won't have much to drink. Anyway, you said you wanted to show your parents you were growing up," said Jenny.

Amrit didn't say anything.

"Come on. Just for an hour," said Jenny.

"Then we'll go to bed."

Amrit still didn't say anything.

"Come on. Say yes," pleaded Jenny.

"Just for one hour?" asked Amrit.

"Just for an hour," said Jenny.

"OK," said Amrit.

They cooked curry from a packet and boiled rice in a bag. By the time they had eaten and washed up, it was 7.00 p.m. It was time to call their parents and tell them they had reached Zennor. Nothing was said about going to the pub.

Then they had a wash in the campsite toilets, put on clean jeans, clean shirts and some make-up.

They were ready to go. As they walked up the road, Amrit said, "I've never been in a pub and ordered drinks before."

"Just act as if you've done it lots of times," said Jenny.

Amrit tried. She walked up to the bar

and said, "Two halves of lager, please."

"Yes, love. Which one?" asked the barman. Amrit froze. She didn't know there were different sorts of lager. She wanted to turn and run. But then she looked at the names on the pumps and said, "Harp, please."

Amrit paid for the drinks and took them outside.

"Your hands are shaking," said Jenny.

"I got a bit frightened in there," said Amrit.

"But you did it. Well done," said Jenny.

The girls only had time for a sip of their drinks before a motorbike screeched to a stop, and the two lads jumped off.

"Well, well. So I *have* got a date," said the blond one.

"No you haven't. We've just come for a drink," said Jenny.

He took off his helmet and sunglasses.

"My name's Dean," he said. He held out his hand for Amrit to shake.

"I'm Amrit," she said.

"And I'm Jenny," she said, as she shook his hand.

Dean held onto Jenny's hand. "How do you like my bike? I call it my Mean Machine," he said.

Jenny could feel herself starting to blush, but she didn't try to take her hand away.

"Who's your friend?" asked Amrit.

Dean let go of Jenny's hand and pointed to his mate. "This is Ricky. He's very shy. He doesn't know what to say to girls. Do you Ricky?" Ricky looked down at the ground.

"Hello, Ricky," said Amrit. She reached out her hand for him to shake. Jenny did the same.

Dean said, "Well. Now we know each other, let's get on with the date."

"It's not a date and we're going in an hour," said Amrit.

Dean winked at Jenny, and said, "We haven't got much time then, have we?"

Jenny felt herself blushing again. She'd never been spoken to like this before.

"Come on. Let's see what's going on in the Games Room," said Dean.

He grabbed Jenny by the hand and led her to a room at the back of the pub.

"Be careful. I'm spilling my drink," she said. Amrit and Ricky followed on behind them.

The Games Room had a jukebox, a slot machine, a dartboard and a pool table.

Dean put some money in the jukebox. Then he said, "How about a game of pool?"

"I'm no good at it," said Jenny.

"Play with me and I'll show you how to get better," said Dean, with a big smile on his face.

Ricky put some money into the slot and the balls rolled out. Dean set the balls up on the table and took the first shot.

He hit the cue ball as hard as he could into the pack. The balls scattered all over the table.

Ricky let Amrit play next. She'd played pool before and was quite good. She got a ball into a side pocket. Her next shot just missed.

"Your go, Jenny," said Dean.

"I don't know how to hold the stick," she said. Dean stood behind her, put his arms round her, and took hold of her hands.

"It's called a cue. Let me show you how to play the shot," he said.

Jenny didn't say no. She liked him being this close. She could feel his leather jacket and smell his aftershave.

Dean moved her right hand backwards and forwards so she got used to it.

"Just keep your eye on the ball, and play the shot smoothly," he said. Then he let go of her. "Go on. Try the shot yourself."
Jenny hit the ball but missed the pocket.

"Not bad. You just need some more of my help," said Dean. Jenny giggled and started blushing again. Ricky went next, and potted three balls.

"Well played," said Amrit.

"Thanks," said Ricky. It was the first time he had spoken to her.

More shots were taken. More money went into the jukebox and Dean got more drinks.

"We were only having one drink," said Amrit.

"Go on. One more won't harm you. We haven't finished the game yet," said Dean.

Jenny took her next shot and got a ball into a side pocket. She jumped up and down with joy, shouting, "I got one in!"

Dean gave her a hug. Then he lifted her off the ground and swung her round.

"What a shot. I knew you could do it," he said. Then he gave her a quick kiss on the cheek.

"Hey, you. Cut that out," said Jenny. But she was smiling as she said it.

Amrit didn't look so happy.

"We should be going back soon," she said.

"Not yet. Not when I'm just getting the hang of this game," said Jenny.

Jenny missed her next shot. Now it was Ricky's shot. He needed to pot the last two balls and the black ball to win the game. He did it! Dean groaned and then swore.

Jenny said, "Well I want another game."

"So do I. They can't get that lucky again," said Dean.

He quickly put more coins in the slot.

As Dean set up the table for another game, Amrit came over to speak to Jenny.

"We agreed to go back in an hour," she said.

"It won't take long to play a game," said Jenny.

"What game are we talking about?" asked Amrit. Jenny looked puzzled.

"You know what I mean. It's not just a game of pool that Dean's after," said Amrit.

Jenny looked shocked. "It's just a bit of fun," she said.

"Well, let's hope it stays like that," said Amrit.

"Oh, shut up. You sound just like my dad," said Jenny.

Dean fed the jukebox with money. Jenny started dancing to the music. Ricky got more drinks and Amrit started the next game.

Chapter 5

It wasn't long before Dean and Jenny were spending more time fooling around than playing pool.

Then they started dancing. Ricky and Amrit got fed up and sat down.

With two drinks inside him, Ricky started to talk more. He told Amrit about the rock climbing and sea fishing he did with his dad.

Amrit told him about the backpacking trip.

Dean was doing some talking as well. "How about you and me sneaking off and going for a ride?" he asked Jenny, as they danced.

"I've never been on a bike," said Jenny.

"There's got to be a first time for everything," smiled Dean.

"I think I'd be a bit frightened," said Jenny.

"All you've got to do is put your arms round me and hang on," said Dean. Jenny giggled and swayed a little.

"But I haven't got a helmet," she said.

"I've got two," said Dean.

"Lucky you," smiled Jenny.

"I keep them under my seat," said Dean.

"Best place for them," giggled Jenny.

"Well, how about it?" asked Dean.

"I can't just leave Amrit," said Jenny.

Dean spotted Amrit going off to the toilet.

"Then don't tell her," he said. He grabbed hold of Jenny's hand and ran out of the pub. He lifted her onto the back of his bike and put a helmet on her head. After two kick-starts the bike roared into life.

"Hang on. Here we go!" yelled Dean. Jenny was holding onto Dean's jacket but almost fell off as the bike shot off up the road. She quickly put her arms round Dean and gripped the seat with her knees.

"You're going too fast!" she shouted in his ear.

"I can't hear you," he lied. He went even faster. Then he leaned the bike over as he raced into the first bend. Jenny felt as if she was falling off so she leaned the other way.

"Lean the same way I do. Lean into the bend, not away from it," shouted Dean. Jenny tried, as they went round bend after bend. Then they came to a hump-back bridge.

"Oh, no!" she screamed, as the bike took off and flew through the air.

As they came thumping back down onto the road, Dean had to work hard to keep the bike upright. But he didn't slow down. Jenny felt frightened, excited and sick, all at the same time.

After two more bends they came to a turning. They went left and joined a long line of traffic that was being held up by a slow-moving tractor. A stream of cars, buses and lorries were coming the other way. Jenny began to relax.

At least Dean would have to slow down and stay in line. But he didn't.

He aimed the bike down the middle of the road. The gap was too small and the oncoming traffic had to pull over to the left. "Hang on!" he yelled.

Cars flashed their lights. Vans sounded their horns.

Drivers swore and shook their fists at him.

Dean kept weaving his way down the line of traffic until he overtook the tractor. "Yes! It's the Mean Machine in the lead again," he shouted.

After a few more bends he turned left down a narrow lane, and began slowing down.

"You can stop pushing your head into my back, now," he said. Jenny sat up and opened her eyes.

As soon as they stopped, she punched Dean in the back. Then she jumped off the bike.

"You're mad. You could have got us killed back there!" she shouted, taking off her helmet.

Dean got off the bike and rested it on its stand. Then he took off his helmet. "But I didn't. And it was fun," he said.

"No, it wasn't," said Jenny. She was trying to be angry but a smile crept onto her face. Dean put his arms round her and kissed her. After a few seconds she pushed him away.

"I didn't say you could do that," she said.

"I didn't ask," said Dean. He kissed her again. This time she didn't push him away. She'd never been kissed like this before, and she liked it.

When they stopped, Dean said, "How about a walk in the woods?" Before Jenny could say anything, Dean kissed her again. Then he slid his hand inside her jacket.

Jenny didn't know what to do. She'd never felt like this about a boy before. She let his hand stay where it was.

"Come on. Let's go for a walk," said Dean.

"I don't know," said Jenny.

"Come on. It'll be OK. I've got something with me," said Dean. He took hold of Jenny's hand.

"Why can't we just stay kissing?" asked Jenny.

"I know something better than that," said Dean

"I've only just met you," said Jenny.

"Well, come and get to know me a bit better," he said.

Jenny needed time to think. "Look, you're rushing me. Why can't we just stay here?" she said.

"We'll have more fun in the woods. Come on. You know you want to," said Dean. He tried pulling Jenny along with him.

"No. Stop it," she said.

Dean was getting fed up. "What do you mean, stop it? You've been leading me on all night," he said.

"I have not," said Jenny.

"Yes, you have. And you know it," said Dean.

"I just thought it was a bit of fun," said Jenny.

"It is. So why stop now?" said Dean. He pulled Jenny closer to the path.

"I just need some time to think," said Jenny.

"Time's run out," said Dean. He lifted her off the ground and started walking up the path. Jenny was now very frightened and she started slapping him around the head.

"Put me down. Put me down, now," she said. As Jenny tried to get away, she saw a man and a woman coming down the lane with a dog.

"If you don't put me down, I'm going to shout rape. Those people will help me," she said.

Dean turned and looked up the lane. Then he put Jenny back on her feet. The dog came over and Jenny made a fuss of it.

The woman called to the dog. Then she came across and looked at Dean.

"It's Dean, isn't it? I used to work with your dad," she said.

"Yes. We've just come out for a ride on the bike. We're just off back to the pub," he said.

"Right," said the woman. But she and the man didn't walk on until Dean and Jenny were on the bike and going down the lane.

Dean turned and shouted to Jenny, "All right slag, I'll take you back. At least I'll get a drink."

Jenny hated that word. She'd never been called it before. Tears filled her eyes. It wasn't fair. How could someone kiss her and make her feel so good and then treat her like that? She cried all the way back.

Dean took a short cut and they were soon back outside the pub. Amrit and Ricky were waiting for them.

Jenny got off the bike and threw the crash helmet at Dean. She was hoping he'd say sorry, but he didn't. He didn't say a word. So she walked off down the road.

Amrit ran after her. "Where have you been? What happened?" she asked.

"Nothing happened," said Jenny.

"You've been crying," said Amrit.

"So what. Lots of people cry. Just leave me alone. I want to go to bed," said Jenny.

It was 10 p.m. when they got to the tent. Just as they were getting into their sleeping bags, Amrit's phone started ringing. She told her dad they were both OK.

Then she curled up in her sleeping bag, and listened to Jenny cry herself to sleep.

Chapter 6

"Come on. Time to get up," said Amrit, from outside the tent. She got hold of one of Jenny's feet and gave it a shake. Jenny made a groaning noise, but didn't move. "Come on. We've got some walking to do today," said Amrit.

"I don't feel well. My head hurts," said Jenny.

"It's called a hangover," said Amrit.

"Can't we stay here for the day?" asked Jenny.

"No. Come on. There's a mug of tea waiting for you out here," said Amrit.

"I want my tea in my sleeping bag," said Jenny.

"You can't drink out of a sleeping bag," said Amrit.

"Very funny. I mean, I'll stay in my sleeping bag and drink out of the mug," said Jenny.

"No. You can't do that," said Amrit.

"Why not?" asked Jenny.

"Because I'm not passing it to you," said Amrit.

"Please, please, please," pleaded Jenny.

"No, no, no," said Amrit. Jenny swore at her.

"That's not nice," said Amrit.

"I hate you," said Jenny.

But she got out of her sleeping bag, put on some shorts and a T-shirt, and crawled out of the tent.

"The sun's too bright," she said.

"Oh, I'm sorry. I'll turn it down," said Amrit. Jenny gave her a 'drop dead' look. Then she drank some tea. "Mmm. That's better. What time is it?"

"8 a.m.," said Amrit.

"8 a.m.! We could have had two more hours in bed," shouted Jenny.

"No, we couldn't. We've got to have breakfast, pack everything up, get food from the shop and get walking," said Amrit.

"Why can't we have a day off?" asked Jenny.

"Do you want to stay around here, after last night?" asked Amrit.

Jenny's face turned to stone.

"No, I don't," she said.

Two hours later, they were walking out of the village. Jenny was hoping they wouldn't see Dean. They didn't.

As they reached the coast path, Amrit asked, "Are you all right?"

"No. My head hurts. My legs hurt and I feel upset about last night," said Jenny.

"Do you want to talk about it?" asked Amrit.

"I don't want to talk about boys, or see any boys, ever again," said Jenny.

"Well, we won't see any tonight. We're going to camp out on the cliff tops," said Amrit.

"Good," said Jenny. And she walked off along the path. Amrit let her go.

For the first hour they walked apart. Amrit was enjoying the walking. She had never felt as free as this. She had everything she needed on her back, and she was seeing new things round every bend.

The sea and sky were a bright blue and there were all sorts of butterflies and flowers.

For Jenny, the walking was helping her sort things out in her mind. Maybe she had drunk too much. But he had no right to act like he did. He should have left her alone when she told him to stop. She would never forget the name he called her.

After an hour's walking she was feeling much better. She waited for Amrit, and said, "To hell with boys. They're all the same. Who needs them?"

"I agree. They're a waste of space," said Amrit.

Jenny said, "They've got so many things wrong with them, they need rubbing out and making again."

"You could make a list of all the things wrong with them," said Amrit. The girls looked at each other.

"Let's do it," they said. As they walked along, they made up a list called,

'All You Need To Know About Boys'.
   They smell.
   They pee on toilet seats.
   They fart in class.
   They can only talk in football lingo.
   They've got dirty minds.
   They're always showing off.
   They're spotty.
   They're always scratching their_____.

They laughed so much they almost wet themselves. It made them forget about the steep hills.

At lunchtime, they sat overlooking a small sandy bay. The sun was hot but a cool breeze was coming in from the sea. They made sandwiches and ate them. They drank cans of cola too quickly, which made them burp.

"How much further to go?" asked Jenny.

"About four miles. I'm hoping we can camp this side of that lighthouse," said Amrit, pointing down the coast.

After a long sit in the sun, and a cool drink of water, the girls set off walking again.

Amrit kept checking her map, just to see where they were. She had always liked maps, and she loved some of the names on this walk. There was Mussel Point, Wicca Pool, Porthglaze Cove, Robin's Rocks, Great Zawn and Brandy's Rocks.

The names made her think of smugglers' caves and coves. Of shipwrecks on stormy nights. Of lifeboats battling against angry seas. Of brave fishermen risking their lives to make a living.

"You won't catch me doing that," said Jenny. The words jolted Amrit from her thoughts.

Jenny was watching four rock climbers inching their way up the cliff. It made Amrit think of Ricky. Why did he hang out with a prat like Dean?

"Would you have a go at that?" asked Jenny

"I might do, if I could trust the person I was climbing with," said Amrit.

"Well it sends shivers up and down my spine just watching them," said Jenny.

They walked on. By 4 p.m. they had reached the spot where Amrit had planned to camp for the night. The only good bit of ground for the tent was close to the edge of the cliff.

"We'd better put the tent facing away from the edge. Then if we go for a pee in the night, we won't fall over the cliff," said Jenny.

That set them off laughing, and the tent took ages to put up.

Then Amrit said, "Right. We've only got a drop of water left. We need some for tonight's cooking and tomorrow's breakfast. We also need full bottles for tomorrow's walking."

"Where can we get it from?" asked Jenny.

Amrit pointed to a path going inland. "There's a small village over there," she said.

"You mean more walking?" asked Jenny.

"Without water, we've got no walking holiday," said Amrit.

"You call this a holiday?" asked Jenny.

"Stop moaning," said Amrit.

"I'm not moaning, I'm just saying," said Jenny.

"Come on. It won't take us long. We don't need to take our big packs with us," said Amrit.

They put everything in the tent and

zipped it up. Then they set off up the path with their water bottles, and a big plastic water container that Amrit kept folded up in her rucksack.

They found a public toilet with a drinking water tap outside. Then they struggled back to the tent with plenty of water. They cooked and ate a meal, washed up, and gave their parents a call.

From the top of the cliff, they sat watching the sun go down. It was a great sight, as the huge ball of fire seemed to slip slowly into the sea. The sky changed from blue, to pink, to red. Then darkness took over, and one by one the stars began to shine.

With no streetlights, the stars looked brighter than they had ever looked before. There were soon thousands of them, filling the sky with dots of light.

"I've never seen a sky like this. How many stars do you think there are?" asked Jenny.

"I haven't got a clue," said Amrit.

"Well, how far away are they?" asked Jenny.

"Light years," said Amrit.

"What do you mean, light years?" asked Jenny.

"It's the number of miles light can travel in a year," said Amrit.

"So, those stars could be millions of miles away?" said Jenny.

"Yes," said Amrit.

"So how big is space?" asked Jenny.

"I don't think anyone knows," said Amrit.

"I mean, how far is it to the end of space?" asked Jenny.

"I don't think there is an end," said Amrit.

"But it's got to end somewhere," said Jenny.

"I think it just keeps going forever," said Amrit.

"Forever! It can't go on forever. I can't get my head round that," said Jenny.

"Nor can I," said Amrit. They sat staring up at the stars until their necks hurt. Then they both shivered with cold.

Snuggled up in their sleeping bags, they went on talking. At last, Jenny told Amrit everything that had happened with Dean.

"All he wanted was sex," said Jenny.

"Maybe that's what they all want," said Amrit.

"Well I hope some of them are better at asking," said Jenny.

"Does your dad ask your mum?" asked Amrit.

"Oh please. Let's not go there," said Jenny. The giggling started.

"Mine still do it. I've heard them," said Amrit.

"Oh, that's gross. You'd think they'd stop at their age," said Jenny.

The giggling went on.

"So, was Dean good at kissing?" asked Amrit.

"Yes, but it felt like he was trying to eat me at one point," said Jenny.

"Maybe he thought you were a tart," said Amrit.

"Oh, very clever. Thank you very much," said Jenny. But now, she could laugh about it.

At last the giggling turned to sleeping. And the only noise was the sea crashing onto the rocks.

Chapter 7

It was 4 a.m. A sea fog had come in with the tide. The foghorn at the lighthouse began blasting out its warning. The girls were suddenly awake.

"That's going to drive me mad," said Amrit.

"So why did we camp so close to it?" asked Jenny.

"I didn't know the the fog was going to come in," said Amrit.

They drifted in and out of sleep for the next four hours. Then it was time to get up, eat up and pack up.

As they set off for another day's walking, Amrit said, "This is going to be boring. We're not going to see a thing in this fog. I can't even see the sea."

"I can see a flashing light and hear a loud noise," said Jenny.

"Thank you. That's very helpful," said Amrit.

They plodded on with a blanket of wet fog all around them. The foghorn was getting louder as they got closer to it. As they went past the lighthouse, the fog lifted just a little.

"Is that a chimney over there?" asked Jenny.

"Yes. There were tin mines around here

but they've all gone now," said Amrit.

For the next two hours they walked on old mining ground. They went past tumbled-down walls, broken trucks, old wheels and deep holes in the ground. They saw bits of broken rail and steel rope.

Amrit found part of an old clay pipe. The fog made it all feel spooky. Maybe they'd see the ghost of the old miner come walking out of the fog, looking for his pipe?

"What do you think it was like underground?" asked Amrit.

"There's an information board over there," said Jenny.

The board told them that a miner had a 300-metre climb down ladders to the bottom of the shaft. Then an 800-metre scramble under the seabed to get to the rock face. He only had a candle to light his way!

For six hours a day he would cut, and hack, and dig. Sometimes kneeling down, sometimes flat on his back. After six hours he was soaked with sweat and gasping for air. Then he had the long scramble back.

"Look here," said Jenny. "It says children worked down there. Some of them were only eight years old."

"I'll never bitch about having to go to school, again," said Amrit. They walked on to the top of the next hill.

Then they stopped for a rest and took off their packs. It was 11 a.m., and they sat watching the sun burning the fog off the hills.

"Thank goodness for that," said Amrit.

Jenny looked at the path stretching ahead of them. "So, we walk to a campsite just past Cape Cornwall and stay there tonight. Then tomorrow, Mum and Dad pick us up from there. Is that right?," she asked.

"That's it," said Amrit.

"So how far is it to the campsite?"

asked Jenny.

"About another five miles," said Amrit.

"I hope we get there in time for a swim in the sea," said Jenny.

"You just want to show off your new bikini," said Amrit.

"Well, I've got more to show than you," said Jenny as she pushed out her chest.

"Not much you haven't, you cheeky cow," said Amrit.

"And you're a rat-face," said Jenny.

"Dingbat," said Amrit.

"Dippy cat," said Jenny.

"Old hag," said Amrit, starting to smile.

"Old bag," said Jenny, starting to laugh.

"Bitch," said Amrit, giggling.

"Witch," said Jenny, laughing out loud.

By now, they couldn't think of any more insults because they were laughing so much.

Then Jenny said, "Loose woman."

"Loose woman? What's a loose woman? Does she walk like this?" asked Amrit. And she walked around with her arms, legs and head flopping about as if they were going to fall off.

"Loose woman is what my gran calls a woman who runs after a man," said Jenny.

"There's no one here like that, is there?" said Amrit.

They looked at each other and started laughing again. At last the laughing stopped and they wiped the tears from their eyes.

"I'm worn out," said Jenny, laying back in the sun and closing her eyes.

Amrit stood up and put on her pack. She looked down at Jenny and said, "Well, come on, big boobs. If you want a swim, let's get going."

"Armpit!" Jenny shouted after her.

Chapter 8

By 2 p.m. they were standing next to the
tea van in the car park at Cape Cornwall.
They were eating cake and drinking tea.
By 3 p.m. they had reached the path that
went inland to the campsite.

"It's a mile to the campsite. Do we swim
now, or put the tent up and come back?"
asked Amrit.

"Swim now. I'm hot, sweaty and tired. I want to get in that sea as fast as I can," said Jenny.

Waiting for the tide to turn would have been a better plan.

Just ahead of them was a small sandy cove. Jenny led the way down the steep path.

"This is what I've been waiting for," she said.

Finding somewhere to get changed was easy. Big rocks were close by and the only people around were at the far end of the cove.

"Will the packs be safe here?" asked Amrit.

"Would *you* want to nick a heavy pack full of sweaty socks and pants?" asked Jenny.

Amrit was changed before Jenny had even found her bikini in her pack.

"See you, slowcoach," she said.

She jogged across the sand and then sprinted into the sea. She gave a loud scream as cold water splashed over her. Then she dived in and swam out a little way. She looked back to see how Jenny was getting on. And there she was, chatting to a boy!

Amrit smiled. "That girl could find a boy in a Christmas Cracker," she said to herself.

So as Amrit floated on the sea, Jenny flirted on the beach.

At last, Jenny walked into the sea. Amrit heard her short, sharp shouts as the cold water moved slowly up her body.

Amrit turned over and shouted, "Race you to the rocks." She set off for the rocks at the end of the cove. She knew Jenny would catch her because she was a stronger swimmer. But it would be fun trying to beat her.

Amrit put her head down and swam as fast as she could. When she looked up, the rocks looked closer, and Jenny didn't seem to be catching her.

"I can do this," she said.

The next time she looked up there were about 30 metres to go, but Jenny was catching her.

"Come on, one last push," she said.

Amrit kicked hard with her legs and pulled with her arms. She was getting more and more tired. She looked up, hoping to see the rocks just ahead of her. But they weren't. They were still about 30 metres away.

At first, Amrit couldn't understand it. She swam hard again, but something seemed to be stopping her getting any closer.

Then, bit-by-bit, she felt herself being dragged away from the rocks.

She kept on swimming, but it was no good. She was being pulled out to sea.

Now she knew what was happening. This was a rip tide! Strong currents were sweeping her out to sea where she would get cold and tired. And then drown. Swimmers died every year around this coast.

Amrit looked around for help, but she had been swept around the headland. No one in the cove could see her.

Fear gripped hold of her.

"This can't be happening to me. How can I be having fun one minute, and fighting for my life the next?" she said to herself.

But the fight was on. The sea had got her in its grip, and it wasn't going to let her go.

As the rip tide took her out to sea, the waves got bigger and began smashing into her face. She was tired, frightened and struggling to breathe.

She began to panic.

The panic started in her belly and spread to every part of her body. She began thrashing about in the water and yelling for help. But all she got was a mouthful of seawater. She spat it out and tried to breathe, but more and more water got in.

She began to choke and go under. She tried again and again to get her head above water. But it was getting too painful to keep on fighting.

The sea was winning.

"I'm going to die," she said to herself. And she went under for the last time.

Then a hand grabbed her by the hair and yanked her head out of the water.

"Come on. Keep fighting. Get onto your back. Get some air in your lungs!" yelled Jenny.

She rolled Amrit over onto her back. Then she put one hand under her back and the other hand under her chin.

Amrit spluttered, coughed up and spat out as much water as she could.

At last, she got some air into her lungs.

"We can't swim against this tide. All we can do is stay afloat. Stay on your back, and let's hope someone sees us," shouted Jenny.

Amrit looked up at the blue sky and kept trying to breathe. It was like being born again.

But staying afloat wasn't easy. The cold was getting into their bones, and the waves bashed them around even more.

If they didn't get picked up soon, the rip tide would have two more victims. The chances of being seen in a sea like this were very small.

But today, luck was on their side.

As the rip tide took them out to sea, it also took them closer to a small fishing boat. Just as they began crying from fear and cold, they were plucked from the sea by two fishermen. The fishermen put coats and blankets around them.

When Ricky and his dad had set off to go fishing that day, they hadn't expected their catch to be two half-drowned girls.

"Did you swim out from the cove?" asked Ricky's dad.

The girls nodded but couldn't speak. They were shaking with cold, and shocked at how close they had been to drowning.

"You're OK now," said Ricky, as he sat down next to them. It was only then that Amrit saw who it was and she hugged him.

As soon as the boat reached the beach, Ricky and his dad walked and jogged life back into the girls. Dry clothes and a hot sun did the rest.

"I'm very thirsty," said Amrit.

"So am I," said Jenny.

"Go and get that bottle of water from the boat, Ricky," said his dad.

"Don't bring the flask of tea. They shouldn't be having hot drinks yet."

Ricky was soon back with the water. It was the best drink the girls had ever had.

"Now," said Ricky's dad, as he took a mobile out of his pocket, "it's time you called your parents and asked them to pick you up."

"No," said Amrit, quickly.

Ricky's dad didn't look pleased. "Why not?" he asked.

"If we do that, they'll never let us go off on our own again," said Amrit.

"Maybe that's not a bad thing," he said.

Ricky said, "Dad, you're always telling me it's time I learnt to stand on my own two feet."

"But these are just lasses," said his dad.

The girls looked at each other.

Ricky said, "Times have changed, Dad. It's just the same for girls."

Ricky's dad looked at the three of them. At last he said, "OK, no phone call. But we'll take you back to the campsite. Then we'll come back later and take you to a doctor. Just for a check-up. Then we'll go for fish and chips."

The girls didn't argue.

Ricky and his dad took them to the campsite and helped put up the tent.

"We'll be back in just over an hour. If you start feeling cold, get into your sleeping bags," said Ricky's dad.

But the girls sat in the sun feeling warm, safe and happy.

"Thanks for saving me, Jenny. How did you know what to do?" said Amrit.

"I used to go to the swimming club at school. It just seemed to come back to me," said Jenny.

"What shall we tell our parents?" said Amrit.

"Not a lot. Let's get them used to us going off on our own. Then we'll tell them," said Jenny.

Amrit smiled. "That's fine with me," she said.

So they called their parents about being picked up in the morning, but didn't tell them about the swim. That could wait for a year or two.

Then Ricky and his dad drove up. Ricky's 17-year-old-brother, Mark, was also in the car.

They took the girls to the doctor for a check-up.

Then they went for fish, chips and mushy peas. By the time Jenny had finished her meal she was in love again!

"I hope your swim hasn't put you off coming to Cornwall," said Mark.

"Oh no. We're planning another walking holiday down here. Aren't we, Amrit?" said Jenny.

"Yes, we are," said Amrit, as she and Ricky held hands under the table.

Look out for other exciting stories in the
Survival series:

Runaway
The Boss
The Gambling Habit
Stormy Waters
Flirting with Danger
Fireproof
Why Me?
Jet Scream

About the author

Have you ever been hunted by the police, chased by a gang, or tried to stay alive after a plane crash?

If you have, then you know the name of the game is survival. If you haven't, why not read about the teenagers in my stories. They find getting into trouble is easy. It's the getting out of trouble that's the hard bit.

I spent three years training to be a teacher and 33 years being one. I always wanted to know how hard it would be to write books for teenagers. Now I know!

Pete Guppy

SURVIVAL

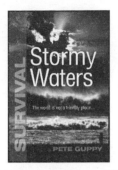
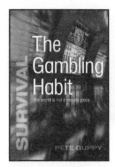

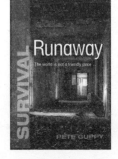

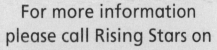